MW01107835

NATURE MANDALA

Colouring Book
For Adults

Om Books International

Reprinted in 2022

Corporate & Editorial Office
A-12, Sector 64, Noida 201 301
Uttar Pradesh, India
Phone: +91 120 477 4100
Email: editorial@ombooks.com
Website: www.ombooksinternational.com

Sales Office
107, Ansari Road, Darya Ganj
New Delhi 110 002, India
Phone: +91 11 4000 9000
Email: sales@ombooks.com
Website: www.ombooks.com

© Om Books International 2017

ALL RIGHTS RESERVED. No part of this book may be reproduced or
transmitted in any form by any means, electronic or mechanical, including
photocopying and recording, or by any information storage and retrieval
system, except as may be expressly permitted in writing by the publisher.

ISBN: 978-93-85609-73-2

Printed in India

10 9 8 7 6 5 4 3 2

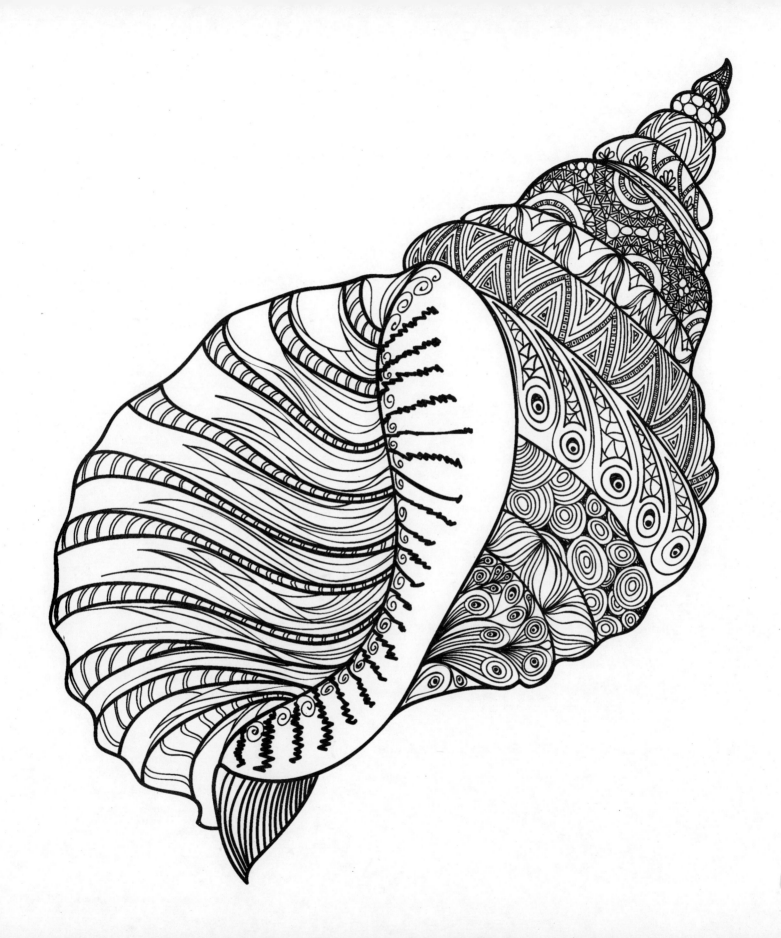

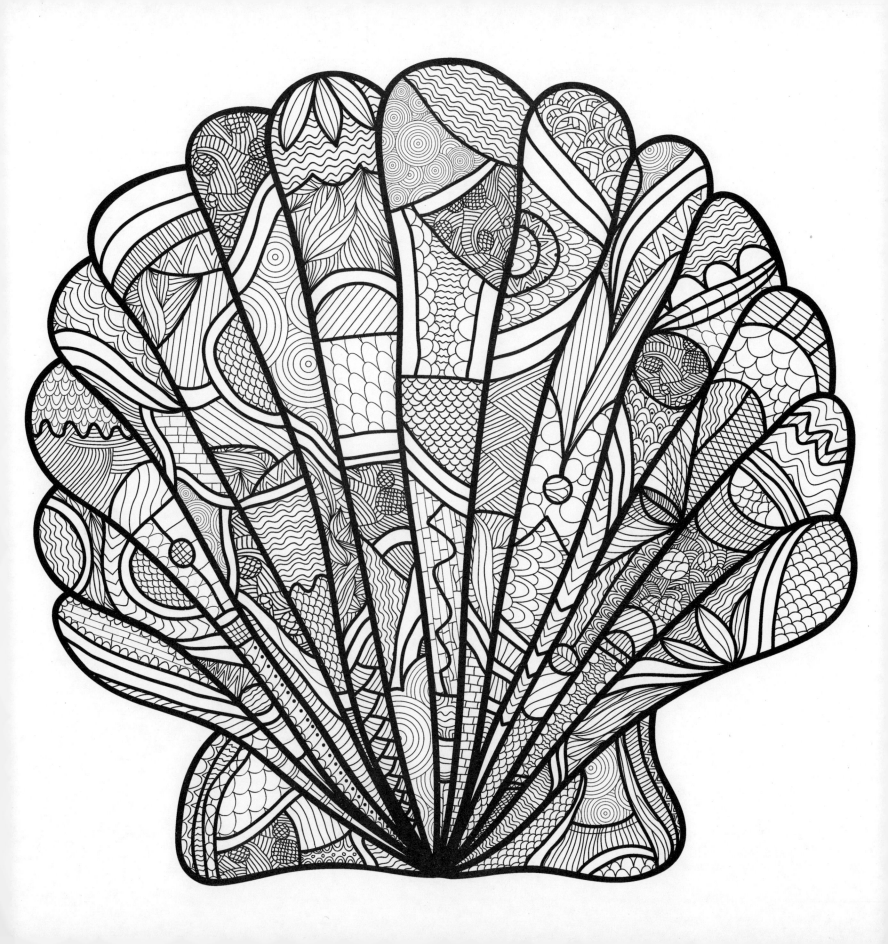